Slithering Snakes
BLACK Mambas

by Julie Murray

Dash!
LEVELED READERS
1

Dash!
LEVELED READERS

Level 1 – Beginning
Short and simple sentences with familiar words or patterns for children who are beginning to understand how letters and sounds go together.

Level 2 – Emerging
Longer words and sentences with more complex language patterns for readers who are practicing common words and letter sounds.

Level 3 – Transitional
More developed language and vocabulary for readers who are becoming more independent.

abdopublishing.com
Published by Abdo Zoom, a division of ABDO, P.O. Box 398166, Minneapolis, Minnesota 55439.
Copyright © 2018 by Abdo Consulting Group, Inc. International copyrights reserved in all countries.
No part of this book may be reproduced in any form without written permission from the publisher.

Printed in the United States of America, North Mankato, Minnesota.
092017
012018

Photo Credits: Alamy, Animals Animals, iStock, Minden Pictures, Science Source, Shutterstock
Production Contributors: Kenny Abdo, Jennie Forsberg, Grace Hansen, John Hansen
Design Contributors: Dorothy Toth, Neil Klinepier

Publisher's Cataloging in Publication Data
Names: Murray, Julie, author.
Title: Black Mambas / by Julie Murray.
Description: Minneapolis, Minnesota: Abdo Zoom, 2018. | Series: Slithering snakes |
    Includes online resource and index.
Identifiers: LCCN 2017939237 | ISBN 9781532120718 (lib.bdg.) | ISBN 9781532121838 (ebook) |
    ISBN 9781532122392 (Read-to-Me ebook)
Subjects: LCSH: Black Mamba--Juvenile literature. | Snakes--Juvenile literature. | Reptiles--Juvenile
    literature.
Classification: DDC 597.964--dc23
LC record available at https://lccn.loc.gov/2017939237

THIS BOOK CONTAINS
RECYCLED MATERIALS

Table of Contents

Black Mambas

Black mambas are deadly!
They are found in Africa.

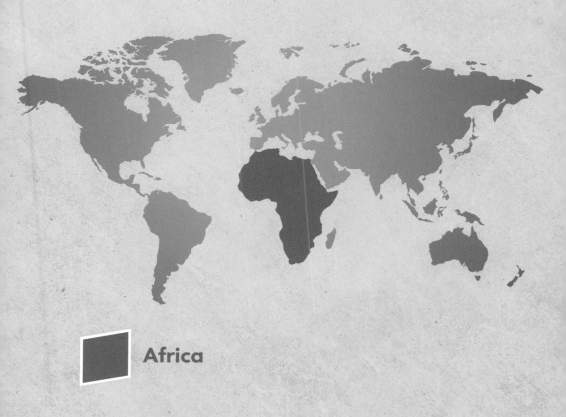

Africa

They live on grassy **plains**.

They also live on rocky hills.

They have long, thin bodies.
They can be more than
10 feet (3.0 m) long!

They are gray or
brown in color.

The inside of their mouth is black. This is how they got their name.

They have two **fangs**.
The fangs release a
deadly **venom**.

Black mambas bite their **prey**.

They wait for it to die.
They eat it whole.

They eat mice and squirrels.
They also eat birds.

They can live for
11 years in the wild.

More Facts

- Black mambas can move fast. They can reach speeds of 7 miles per hour (11 kph)!

- Two drops of their **venom** can kill a human.

- They are the longest venomous snakes found in Africa.

Glossary

fang – a long, pointed tooth that is used to bite prey and inject venom.

plain – a large, flat area of land with very few trees.

prey – an animal that is hunted and eaten by another animal.

venom – the poison that certain snakes produce.

Index

Online Resources

Booklinks
NONFICTION NETWORK
FREE! ONLINE NONFICTION RESOURCES

To learn more about black mambas, please visit **abdobooklinks.com**. These links are routinely monitored and updated to provide the most current information available.